How Beautiful

Antonella Capetti

Illustrated by Melissa Castrillón

GREYSTONE KIDS

GREYSTONE BOOKS • VANCOUVER / BERKELEY

First published in Canada, the U.S., and the U.K. by Greystone Books in 2021
Originally published in Italy in 2017 as *Che bello*
Text and illustrations copyright © 2017 by Topipittori, Milan
Translation copyright © 2021 by Lisa Topi

21 22 23 24 25 5 4 3 2 1

Greystone Kids / Greystone Books Ltd.
greystonebooks.com

Cataloguing data available from Library and Archives Canada

ISBN 978-1-77164-853-0 (cloth)
ISBN 978-1-77164-854-7 (epub)

MIX
Paper from
responsible sources
FSC® C016973

Editing by Kallie George
Copy editing by Doretta Lau
Proofreading by Doeun Rivendell
English text design by Sara Gillingham Studio
The illustrations in this book were drawn in five graphite pencil layers,
which were then scanned and converted to color digitally.
Printed and bound in China by 1010 Printing International Ltd.

This book has been translated thanks to a contribution from
the Ministry of Italian Foreign Affairs and International Cooperation.
Questo libro è stato tradotto grazie a un contributo del
Ministero degli Affari Esteri e della Cooperazione Internazionale italiano.

Greystone Books gratefully acknowledges the Musqueam, Squamish,
and Tsleil-Waututh peoples on whose land our office is located.

Greystone Books thanks the Canada Council for the Arts, the British Columbia Arts Council,
the Province of British Columbia through the Book Publishing Tax Credit,
and the Government of Canada for supporting our publishing activities.

Once, there was a caterpillar.
He was happy on his leaf.
Actually—leaves! There were lots.
Every day he'd sleep, eat,
crawl around, and sleep some more.
It was a good, simple life.
He never questioned anything.

Until one day,
while he was rambling
from leaf to leaf,
he was suddenly
lifted off the ground.
He was hanging by a twig.
He knew twigs very well.
Leaves were often
attached to them.
But this twig didn't have
any leaves and was moving
higher very quickly!

The caterpillar looked up. An Unknown Thing was standing in front of him. It had a strange smell, unlike the usual scent of forest, moss, and wet soil.

"You're so beautiful," the Unknown Thing said. Then it gently laid him and the twig down, and as suddenly as it had arrived, it went away.

Beautiful.

Nobody had ever told the caterpillar
he was beautiful before.

"But what does *beautiful* mean?"
he wondered.

He asked a bear
who padded by.

"Oh, this is beautiful,"
the bear answered, lifting up
a honeycomb between its paws.

"Not at all," a blackbird nearby uttered.
"That's not beautiful. That's tasty.
Honey is tasty to bears, leaves are tasty
to caterpillars, and caterpillars…
are tasty to blackbirds."

The caterpillar quickly
crept backward.

Inside a heap of dry leaves,
three squirrels were
playing hide-and-seek.

"What does beautiful mean?"
the caterpillar asked them.

The squirrels paused.
"Oh, these dry leaves are beautiful!"
one of them cried out, and they all
started rolling and hiding again.

"No, no," the blackbird said.
"Those are not beautiful.
Those are fun."

The caterpillar moved on.
As it started raining,
he bumped into a mouse.

"Do you know what beautiful means?"
he asked the mouse.

The mouse nodded.
"This mushroom is beautiful!"
The mouse ducked underneath it.

The blackbird broke in right away.
"Oh, no. That's not beautiful.
That's useful..."

"And not to everyone!"
the bear added,
taking cover under
an oak tree.

The rain stopped,
but the caterpillar felt sad.
He used to feel so content.

He used to have no thoughts,
no questions, no worries.
Now, all he wanted was to
find out what beautiful meant.

Then the caterpillar remembered an unusual deer who had moved to the forest recently.

The deer spent most of its time thinking, while resting on a sofa that had been abandoned in the forest.

"The deer must know a lot about beauty," the caterpillar decided.

"Can you tell me what beautiful means?"
the caterpillar asked the deer.

"Of course," the deer answered.
"This seat is beautiful!"

"It is not!" the blackbird said.
"That's comfortable,
but *not* beautiful for sure."

The deer hadn't been able to help after all,
and the caterpillar felt tired now.

If only he could go home to his leaf,
and get rid of the blackbird
and the bothersome question.

But the question wouldn't leave him alone.
All he could do was keep asking and hope
for the right answer.

A mole's face peeked out from a hole.

"Can *you* tell me what's beautiful?"
the caterpillar asked.

"It's very beautiful down here," the mole replied.

Naturally,
the blackbird chimed in,
"It might be warm and
cozy down there,
but I don't think it's
beautiful."

"But what *does* beautiful mean?"
the caterpillar asked the blackbird.
"If you know so much, you should tell me!"

"That's beautiful!" the blackbird
shouted suddenly, wildly lunging
toward an empty can.

"How silly!" the other animals exclaimed.
"That's not beautiful. That's shiny!"

The caterpillar sighed.
Even *he* knew that.
And now night was falling.
He'd never find an answer.

Slowly, the tired animals lay on the ground
with their noses and beaks pointed toward the sky.
The caterpillar looked up, too, and gasped.

"How beautiful!" they all exclaimed.

Beautiful.

The caterpillar smiled.
So it was.